oks by Walter Mosley

vil in a Blue Dress
Red Death
hite Butterfly
ack Betty

vailable from POCKET BOOKS

EVERYONE'S TALKING ABOUT WALTER MOSLEY'S BRILLIANT NEW MYSTERY

a red death

EVERYONE'S TALKING ABOUT
WALTER MOSLEY'S
BRILLIANT CITY MYSTERY

"Walter Mosley is a gifted writer who captures the lingo and culture of the 1950s Watts with skill. . . ."
—*Chattanooga Times*

"Mr. Mosley knows his characters so intimately. . . . At times, several of the urban people in Mr. Mosley's Watts are not far removed from those living in Catfish Row in *Porgy and Bess*. Mr. Mosley has depicted a special locale and a corner-cutting way of life that most readers will find far more riveting than the crime pages of their newspapers."
—*The New York Times Book Review*

"Mosley proves himself a master at delineating the foibles of his characters. The plotting is equally masterful in this earthy story set in 1950s Watts."
—*Indianapolis Star*

"Easy Rawlins returns, full of mystery, misch color. . . . This is a master at work: we would advised to seek everything Walter Mosley writ
—*The Indianapo*

"Easy is the breakthrough character who, like establishes the standard and defines the field Walter Mosley's wonderfully talented hands, 'ta about life' becomes not just a crackling good my but that most elusive of all fiction—art."
—*Oakland Tribune*

"Some crime writers go beyond the murder case at hand to create an entire world, one populated by colorful characters and filled with rich scenes an exotic locales. Walter Mosley is such a writer. budding master who takes us to another time another place and, for many of us, into an skin. . . . Mosley takes you to that world as ef lessly as another writer might lead you acro street. It's a trip you'll want to take again."
—*Albuquerque*